The Unicorns of Blossom Wood

First published in the UK in 2016 by Scholastic Children's Books
An imprint of Scholastic Ltd
Euston House, 24 Eversholt Street
London, NW1 1DB, UK
Registered office: Westfield Road, Southam, Warwickshire, CV47 0RA
SCHOLASTIC and associated logos are trademarks and/or registered
trademarks of Scholastic Inc.

ISBN 978 1407 17122 7

A CIP catalogue record for this book is available from the British Library

Printed and bound by CPI Group (UK) Ltd, Croydon, CR0 4YY
Papers used by Scholastic Children's Books are made from wood
grown in sustainable forests.

1 3 5 7 9 10 8 6 4 2

www.scholastic.co.uk

Catherine Coe

Unicorn games
& quizzes
inside!

The Unicorns of Blossom Wood

Believe in Magic

SCHOLASTIC

Echo Mountains
Badger Falls
Rushing River
Moon Chestnut
Oval of Oaks
The Great Hedge

For Auntie Bina, the most magical of storytellers.

Thank you for all the memories xxx

Thanks to Dina von Lowenkraft for all your

invaluable advice, and to Tom and Abi Holroyde,

my readers down under!

Chapter 1

The Hoof Prints

"That's like the hundredth time you asked that question!"

Lei ignored Ying, and her dad's face appeared in the gap between the seats. "Keep watching, Lei. Look!"

She turned back to the window. As they swung past a bend in the road, a huge field dotted with brightly coloured

tents came into view. The sign by
the entrance read "Hilltop Hideaway".
It sounds magical! thought Lei, as she
scanned the field for her cousins. Was
that Cora she could see jumping out of
a car with a guitar case in the distance?
And Isabelle, trailing a rucksack as she
walked down a gravel path?

eir car bumped along the pebbly

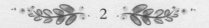

campsite road, all the way to the far edge of the field. Sure enough, there were Lei's aunts and uncle, holding up tent poles and plastic sheets with confused looks on their faces. As soon as the car stopped, Lei unclipped her seat belt and jumped out, and was immediately bowled over by two sets of arms hugging her. She knew who it was without having to look – her cousins, Isabelle and Cora!

"Hurrah, you're here!" shouted Cora. "I can't believe I got here first even though I had to travel the furthest!" Cora lived in Australia with her mum and dad. But the families always spent a week of the summer holidays together, and it was the three girls' favourite time of the year.

"It took AGES to drive here from

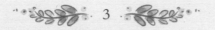

the airport," said Lei. Her family lived
in San Francisco, although her mum
was Chinese and her dad was English.
"Ying was carsick, so we had to keep
stopping!"

Isabelle grinned, and her bright green
eyes flashed like jewels. "But you're here
now. Come on, let's explore!"

Lei looked over at her parents getting

out of the car. "Is it OK if we have a look around?" she asked.

"Go ahead," her mum replied, walking towards the pieces of tent. "This will keep us busy for a while!"

Isabelle's mum nodded, then smiled and passed Lei's mum a giant bunch of tent pegs.

Lei looked at the plastic sheeting strewn across the grass. "Should we help?" she offered.

"No, no," said her dad. "I think we have it covered. Go have fun!"

"Just be back in time for the barbie," Cora's dad added. "I'm doing my special chook sauce!"

The three girls linked arms and skipped across the hilltop field. As they ran down the slope, a circular blue lake set amid grassland came into view.

"I know barbie means barbecue in Australia, but what on earth is a chook?" asked Lei. "It sounds weird!"

Cora laughed. "It's the Australian word for chicken. I guess it is a bit weird. But then don't you call a handbag a purse in America? That's just silly!"

The girls giggled together. Even though they lived on different sides of the world, as soon as they saw each other it was like they'd never been apart.

As they drew closer to the lake, Isabelle flung herself into a cartwheel, kicking up the glistening white sand. When she stood up straight again, her fiery red hair curled out from her head like springs.

Meanwhile, Lei threw off her flip-flops and began sprinting to the water. She might have been the shortest of the three

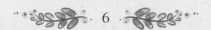

cousins, but she could outrun both of them. "I'm going in," she called over her shoulder. "Who's coming?"

Cora, the tallest, bent down to untie her shoelaces, hearing the splash of the

water and Lei squealing with delight. She took the book she was reading – about a pony school – out of her back pocket and placed it on top of her trainers carefully. Moments later, she was dipping her toe in the water – although Lei and Isabelle were already knee-deep!

"It's freezing!" Cora called, as she hopped on tiptoes towards her cousins. She was used to the warm water of Sydney beaches. This water felt like ice.

"It's fine once you get used to it," said Isabelle, sending a gentle splash Cora's way. Isabelle lived in England, so she was used to paddling in cold sea!

"I agree with Cora," Lei replied. "It's making my feet numb!" Lei started wading back to the shore, her long hair swinging around her shoulders.

Cora followed her cousin out of the

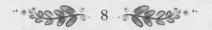

water. "Hey, Lei. What's that in your hair?" she asked, noticing something pink between the silky dark brown strands.

Lei beamed. "Hair braids! Mom did them for me, by wrapping thread around my hair. She wouldn't let me dye my hair pink like Ying," Lei told her cousins. "She says I'm too young. So this was the next best thing!"

"It's ace!" said Cora, picking up a braid and examining it. Then she tugged

at her bobbed blonde hair. "Maybe I can ask Mum to do one for me."

"You should!" said Lei as she shoved her feet back into her pink flip-flops. "Though your hair is pretty as it is."

"What's that over there?" asked Isabelle as she joined them on the sand. She pointed at a cove behind them. It looked like a cave set into the hillside. Around its edge, yellow and purple flowers sprang up among the green grass of the hill. "I wonder what's inside…"

Isabelle skipped up to the cove, beckoning Cora and Lei to follow. "Mum said this area is magical," she told her friends as they walked inside. "Do you think there's magic in here?"

Cora frowned. "I don't think Aunt Phoebe meant real magic, did she?"

Isabelle didn't reply. She was staring

at the rocky ground at the back of the cove. "Are those hoof prints?"

Lei followed her gaze. "Yes!" she said. "But they're really small, like they belong to a pony. Duke's are much bigger." All three of the cousins loved horses and ponies, but Lei was the luckiest because she actually had her own horse!

"But what are they doing in here – in the rock?" Cora ran over and crouched down to look closer.

Lei followed her and gasped. "Hey, look, there are three sets back here. One for each of us!" The other hoof prints were bigger – one set was almost double the size, as if it had been made by a large horse. Lei, who had small feet, jumped into the smallest hoof prints.

Next to her, Isabelle copied Lei, nestling her feet into the medium-sized

set. "You try it too, Cora," Isabelle called over her shoulder.

Cora stood up and put her bare right foot into one of the largest hoof prints, then her left. The rock was smooth, and somehow warm, too. The warmth seemed to shoot through her body – through her legs, stomach, arms and head.

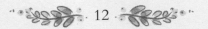

"What's happening?" yelled Lei, as the cove was filled with such dazzling white light that the girls had to close their eyes.

"It's magic, see!" said Isabelle. She squeezed her eyes shut as hot tingles zipped all over her skin.

Something was happening, that was for sure. As the warmth continued to surround her, like the perfect bubble bath, Cora wondered if it really could be magic.

Chapter 2

Blossom Wood

After a few seconds, the bright light began to fade. Lei was the first to open her eyes, and the sight was so shocking, she found she couldn't speak for a moment. She stood on a mountain, with a beautiful woodland landscape stretching out below her – filled with blossoming trees in every direction. She could see a

glimmering lake in the distance, edged by willow trees, and a winding river rushing towards it. Closer by was a tree much taller than the rest, with a curved trunk which Lei thought looked like a crescent moon. The air buzzed with the sound of animals and birds chirping and whistling as they went about their daily business.

"Where ARE we?" Lei asked, looking all around. That was when she noticed something was different. VERY different. Where her feet used to be, there were shiny hooves. And her legs had changed too – they looked like the furry white legs of a horse!

She stumbled backwards – on her hind legs – and saw the backs of two white horses beside her. "C-Cora, Isabelle, is that y-you?!" she stammered.

The two white horses turned around and nodded, their eyes dazzled with shock. But by the look of the horns coming out of her cousins' heads, they weren't horses at all – they were unicorns!

Isabelle, who had a curly, bright red mane and tail, just like her hair, began trotting around. "This is AMAZING!" she cried. "We're unicorns!"

But Cora was shaking her head frantically, making her golden mane swoosh from side to side. "No, no, no – I must be imagining this! It must be the jet lag. It can't be real!"

Lei noticed a shallow pool of water behind them, in the shadows of the mountainside, and had an idea. She nudged Cora towards it. "Look at your reflection. It IS real!"

Cora slowly trotted over to the pool, and Isabelle joined her. The shadows seemed to brighten as the three of them bent their heads to look at the water.

"Magic," Isabelle whispered as three long unicorn heads stared back at them from the pool.

Lei kicked out her front hooves in excitement as she noticed her mane. "I have pink hair!" she cried.

Isabelle pointed her head at Lei's bottom and neighed. "And a pink tail!" Isabelle began trotting along the mountain path, feeling the spring in her step each time her hooves hit the ground. She'd always loved riding ponies – but actually *being* a unicorn was even better. Her white coat seemed to fizz with energy, and she felt warm and happy.

Lei left the pool to follow Isabelle. "Where are we?" she asked again as they cantered along together. It felt strange to be travelling on four legs, but really natural, too – like her legs knew exactly what to do as they moved steadily along the path. "Who do you think lives here?"

Cora galloped towards her cousins and snorted anxiously. "And how will we get back to our families? They'll soon notice we're missing, and we said we'd be back for the barbie!"

Isabelle turned around and trotted back to Cora. "Um, I'm not sure," Isabelle said. "But try not to panic."

Cora had stopped now, her blue eyes clouded with worry, and Isabelle nuzzled her head into her neck to comfort her. As she pulled away, Isabelle spotted something in the rock. "What's that?" she asked, pawing at the ground with her hoof.

Lei galloped over, and saw what Isabelle meant. In the rock, there were more smooth hoof shapes. "Maybe this is how we get home!"

Cora tilted her head, looking unsure. "What do you mean?"

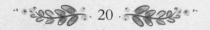

"Well, if we got here by standing in hoof prints," said Isabelle, "we might be able to get back that way too!"

"Maybe you're right…" said Cora, hope fluttering in her chest. "Can we try?"

Lei looked longingly back out at the incredible, inviting view of the forest, but

when she turned and saw Cora shaking with worry, she nodded. She figured they probably *should* check that they could get back OK, although she guessed her parents would still be battling with the tent right now. She jumped into one set of the prints, and Cora and Isabelle quickly did the same. Their hooves fitted each imprint perfectly.

Just as before, warmth spread from their hooves to their legs, bodies and heads, and blinding light made them shut their eyes fast. Heat tingled across their bodies, but it wasn't unpleasant – a bit like sitting in front of a big campfire.

A few seconds later, the warmth and the light disappeared. Cora looked down at herself. "I'm a girl again!" she yelped.

"And we're back at the lake!" Isabelle

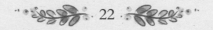

added, pointing towards the still, blue water.

Cora checked her watch, which had musical notes for hands. "It's eight minutes past four. That was the time when we left. It's like time stood still while we were gone!" She walked out of the cove, feeling the soft sand beneath her feet. If she was honest, now that she knew that they could come back, she wanted more than anything to be a unicorn again, and to gallop around in that magical woodland that was waiting to be explored.

Isabelle and Lei were still in the cove with slumped shoulders and downturned mouths. Cora had never seen them look so miserable.

She began heading towards them. "Um ... so shall we go back?" she said tentatively.

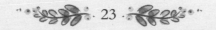

"YES!" they yelled, jumping up and down and beaming.

With Isabelle and Lei still standing in their hoof prints, Cora stepped into hers, and shuddered as the lovely warm feeling flooded through her once again. They

shut their eyes before the light flashed brightly, waiting patiently as their skin tingled with hot magic.

Moments later, they opened their eyes. "We're back," murmured Isabelle. "This is AMAZING."

Lei trotted to the mountain edge and stared at the beautiful view. She raised her head high and turned to her cousins. "I think it's time to explore!"

Chapter 3
Magic Sparks

"Have you seen the sparks?" asked Lei, as she cantered along the path that wound down the side of the mountain.

Cora galloped to catch Lei up, feeling the power in her hind legs each time she pushed off the rock. She had noticed she was taller than Lei and Isabelle – just as she was when they were girls, too. She felt really powerful — as if she had the strength of a racing horse. She wondered just how fast she could run, thinking it would be so much fun to try, although she wouldn't want to leave her cousins behind. "Sparks?" Cora asked. "What do you mean?"

"From our hooves — look!" Lei, who was shorter than Cora — more like a pony — slowed down. Cora did the same, and Isabelle overtook them. Cora watched Isabelle's unicorn hooves hit the ground. As they did, bright red sparkles shimmered upwards, before disappearing like dust in the air.

Cora stopped and stamped a hoof on the ground, and gold sparks flew up around her leg. The gold was the exact colour of her mane and tail. "Unbelievable!"

"Magic!" said Lei. "It's better than any science experiment I've ever done!"

Cora laughed. Lei had blown up her garage more than once with her chemistry experiments that seemed to go wrong more than they went right.

In their last summer holiday, she'd made their caravan stink when she'd tried to make an unbreakable egg. They'd eaten a LOT of omelettes that week.

"What's going on?" Isabelle asked, cantering back to her cousins.

Lei pranced in place, and pink sparks fizzed up from her hooves.

"Oh, wow!" Isabelle tapped her own hooves on the ground and stared at the red sparkles that shone and then disappeared. "I think the sparks must be magical."

"But what do they do?" Lei wondered.

Cora shook her golden mane. "Beats me. Before today I didn't even believe in magic!"

They trotted on along the path, taking in the majestic mountains around them and the vast woodland up ahead. When they reached the bottom of the mountain, Lei spotted a group of pale pink butterflies hovering around a bush. She'd never seen butterflies quite like these before. As they came closer, she thought she could hear whispering, but when she turned to look at Cora and Isabelle, she saw it wasn't her cousins speaking. *Are those butterflies talking?* she wondered, hardly able to believe her ears.

"What's for dinner?" came a little light voice. "I'm fed up with tulip nectar."

"I saw some peaches earlier," said another. "We could try those?"

Lei stopped and stared at the pretty, pale insects. "Hey there, butterflies," she said with a nicker.

The beautiful creatures all turned to look at the unicorns at once. One fluttered out ahead of the others. "Um, hello..." it said uncertainly. "Nice to meet you."

Cora twitched her ears as if she were waving. "G'day. Can you tell us where we are?" she asked.

The butterfly spun around on the spot, as if it was an odd question. "You're in Blossom Wood, of course."

Isabelle grinned. It was the perfect name for the wood, with its blossom-filled trees and bright spring colours.

The butterfly flew closer still, right up to Isabelle's nose. It looked her up and down, and frowned. "Now I have a question for you," it said. "What ARE you?"

Another, bigger, butterfly came to its side. "Yes, please tell us. We've never seen anything like you before!"

Isabelle chewed her lip and glanced across at her cousins. They looked as confused as she felt. "Well, we're

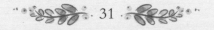

unicorns," she told the butterflies.

At that, all of the butterflies giggled.
Cora thought it sounded like an orchestra
of tiny triangles.

"Don't be silly," said the bigger
butterfly. "Unicorns aren't real!"

Lei stiffened and whinnied. "Of course
they are," she replied. "Look at our horns!"

The first butterfly fluttered backwards and began to shake. "But you can't be! Unicorns don't exist!"

The bigger butterfly looked scared now too. "Come on, let's go. I don't know what you are, but you're fibbing, and fibbers aren't welcome in Blossom Wood!" With that, the frightened butterflies flew up into the blue sky.

"Wait!" called Isabelle, but it was too late. The cousins could only watch as the butterflies disappeared into the distance, blending in with the blossom that fell from the trees.

"What do we do now?" Cora asked quietly. She hadn't expected the creatures here not to believe in unicorns – even if, just a few minutes ago, she hadn't herself!

Lei stamped her front right hoof hard on the ground, making the path tremble. Hundreds of pink sparks flew up, like little tiny fireworks. "Why didn't they believe us?!" She pressed her ears back angrily as heat rose through her body, all the way to the tip of her horn.

Isabelle tossed her head, making her curly red mane bounce about. "I guess they've never seen unicorns before. Maybe we're the only ones in Blossom Wood."

"Maybe," Lei repeated, but her word was drowned out by thunder rumbling in the distance.

Cora tilted her head back and saw heavy grey clouds rushing above them. A bolt of lightning split the sky. "We should shelter," she said, nodding to an overhang at the bottom of the mountain nearby. "That looks perfect."

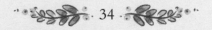

The three cousins galloped to the
shelter of the mountainside. As they
huddled together, Lei felt worry bubble
up inside her. She was so excited about

being in Blossom Wood – and
about being a unicorn. It was like
the best dream ever! But what if the
creatures living here weren't so happy?

Chapter 4
The Search for Friends

The three cousins watched the fat raindrops fall across the wood. *It's beautiful even when it's raining!* thought Isabelle.

Cora pointed her horn towards the horizon. "Look – blue sky." Sure enough, the grey clouds were moving away, and the rain slowed to a quiet patter.

As the sun sparkled its rays down on Blossom Wood once more, Isabelle gasped. "A rainbow!" It arched over the wood, bright and majestic. "What do you think it means?"

Lei turned to Isabelle. "It's the raindrops reflecting the sunlight," she told her. "The water breaks the white light into colours."

Isabelle grinned at her science-crazy cousin. "I know the facts about rainbows – that's not really what I meant. I think it's the wood welcoming us here."

"Really?" Cora raised an eyebrow. "So far, the creatures we've met haven't been exactly friendly."

"That was just those butterflies," Isabelle replied. "Everyone else might be lovely!"

Lei whinnied, flicked her pink tail and trotted away from the mountain. "There's only one way to find out!" she said over her shoulder.

Only a few fluffy white clouds remained in the sky as the cousins

cantered along the woodland trails once more. Lei, with her pony-like legs, had to work hard to keep up with her cousins, whose strides were longer — especially Cora, who powered across the paths without breaking into a sweat.

Isabelle, who was the size and shape of a wild horse, pushed harder with her hind legs to stay close to Cora. Red sparks flew as she felt the exercise heat her body. *I'm going to write about this when we get back*, Isabelle thought. *The bright colours, the sweet, fruit-filled smells of the blossom, the beautiful songs of the twittering birds.* She imagined staying here for ever, as a unicorn. *What would that be like—*

"What's that, to the right?" Lei's voice broke into Isabelle's daydream. Isabelle and Cora followed Lei's gaze — towards a large expanse of flat brown ground. On one edge, a herd of animals roamed around slowly.

"Deer," said Cora, thinking immediately of *Bambi* – one of her favourite books. She switched to a gallop, soon reaching the desert-like area, and heard Lei calling behind her.

"Wait for me!"

Cora skidded to a stop and swung her glossy white head around. Isabelle wasn't too far behind, but Lei was further in the distance – just a dot of white and pink.

"I can't gallop as fast as you!" Lei yelled, tossing her mane in frustration.

Oops, thought Cora. Her American cousin could sometimes be very short-tempered, and Cora didn't want any arguments – not today.

Patiently, she waited for Isabelle and Lei to catch her up. When they were alongside her, all three began moving again – at a trot, this time. They approached the grazing deer.

"Let's be careful," Cora whispered. "I think the best way to get close to a deer is to zigzag towards them."

"Really?" Isabelle said. "Did you see it on TV?"

Cora shook her head. "I read it in a book." The others smiled at that – Cora

had so many books her bedroom was like a library, and when they went on holiday her suitcase always had more books than clothes in it. Not that Isabelle and Lei minded – Cora happily lent them any books they wanted to read. She was like a travelling mini-library!

Lei began to trot in zigzags – left a few paces, right a few paces – and Cora and Isabelle copied. The deer at the front of the herd glanced up for a moment, then went back to nibbling on the grass at the edge of the brown land. Behind this first deer, a smaller one – perhaps her child, thought Lei – looked over. This second deer stared, its brown eyes seeming to grow larger and larger and larger. It poked its head against the belly of its mother, who raised her head once more.

She didn't turn away this time. Instead, she started to bleat loudly. The rest of the deer looked up, let out more bleats ... and the whole herd spun around and raced away, towards the willow-lined lake.

"Wait!" cried Lei. "We won't hurt you!" But the deer didn't look back.

"Should we go after them?" Isabelle wondered, but Cora shook her head.

"If they're scared of us, we'll only frighten them more by chasing them," she said sadly.

Lei neighed. "Come on," she said, trotting in the direction of a river. "Let's find someone else." They crossed the log bridge that made a path over the river and onwards into an apple orchard.

"Look, a squirrel!" whispered Isabelle, spotting one darting down a trunk. But it froze for a split second, stared at the unicorns, then darted back up the trunk again.

Cora groaned. "Everyone's running away!"

They continued through the blossom-covered orchard, seeing birds and insects fluttering between the trees up ahead of them. But every time the unicorns got near, the creatures flew away. "Don't go!" Isabelle cried as a group of little brown birds fled from a nearby branch into the sky.

Lei spotted a little head pop out from a hole in the base of an apple tree trunk. A mouse! She trotted softly over to it and saw there were in fact two mice. They were hugging each other tightly, as if they thought they were about to be eaten.

Lei was about to say hello when they squeaked so loudly Lei wished she had hands to put over her ears. The tiny pair scuttled back into the dark depths of the tree.

Lei shook her head, and cantered to catch up to Isabelle and Cora.

The scrubby woodland path took them

into the cooler surrounds of the pine trees. Isabelle breathed in deeply. The air was thick with the woody scent of the trees.

Lei's ears pricked up – she could hear a scratching sound. She stood on her hind legs and stretched her head up. Her mouth dropped open as she saw the thick black fur of a bear, hugging the tree above her.

"Hello?" Lei said very gently. Cora
and Isabelle stopped too, and quickly saw
what Lei was looking at.

The bear took one arm from the trunk

so it dangled, and glanced down. Isabelle waved a front hoof, trying to show that they were friendly. But the large black animal swung back to the trunk and began shimmying up it faster than Isabelle thought possible.

"Dang!" Cora lowered her head. "It's no good. No one wants to talk to us. Not even the bears. They won't so much as look at us!"

Usually Lei was the most positive of the three, but she had to agree with Cora now. She trembled with frustration, but resisted the urge to stamp her hoof again – that would just frighten the bear more.

"Perhaps we should go home," said Isabelle.

Lei groaned. "I guess no one here has ever met a unicorn, so when they see us they're just scared."

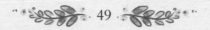

"Like no one at home believes in magic, too," Cora sighed.

Isabelle scanned the sky around them and spotted the tips of the mountains poking out above the treetops. "Come on – I think we can get back that way."

Cora, Lei and Isabelle trotted along in silence, all lost in their own thoughts. Isabelle's stomach swirled with disappointment as she thought about how excited she had been when they'd first arrived here and realized they were unicorns. She blinked, trying to stop her eyes filling with tears, and felt something bump against her leg, accompanied by a deep, croaky shout from the ground.

"Arghhhhhh!"

Chapter 5

Bobby

The three cousins froze mid-trot, and looked down. Something black and furry was huddled in a ball under Isabelle. *Is it a baby bear?* wondered Lei.

"Are you OK?" Cora asked gently, squinting at the animal as it turned its head around, revealing a black-and-white-striped snout. It was a badger!

Isabelle's heart raced with worry. "I think I trod on him!" she cried, bending her head towards the badger. His eyes stared up at her, but he didn't speak.

Lei breathed deeply. "Please say something!" she urged the animal. He opened his mouth slowly, still staring at Lei.

The cousins waited. Wind whistled through the trees, gently rippling their manes and tails.

The badger shut his mouth ... and opened it again.

"I-I'm ... f-fine," he stammered. "B-but w-what are you?"

Cora glanced at Isabelle. If they told him, would he run off like the others?

"We're unicorns," Cora said in her friendliest, most polite voice.

The badger closed his eyes. "I must be dreaming," he said to himself. He had a deep, gravelly voice that rumbled as he spoke. "I've tripped up and hit my head and I'm just imagining things, that's all."

"You're not imagining us," Lei said. "I'm Lei, and this is Isabelle and Cora. We're real," she added softly. She wondered whether to mention that as well as being unicorns, they were girls too – but decided that might frighten him even more.

"*Please* open your eyes," Isabelle said.

The creature gave a little shake of his stripy head and, ever so slowly, opened one eye.

He gulped as he stared at the three animals towering above him. *"Unicorns. Not one, but THREE."*

The cousins nodded and smiled. "We're real," Lei repeated.

"I can see that!" the badger said. "I might be old, but there's absolutely nothing wrong with my eyesight. Yet I thought unicorns were just the stuff of legend..."

"Is that why everyone is scared of us?" Isabelle asked. "All the animals we've met so far have run away!"

The badger rolled over to his front, and tried to push himself upwards. "Oww," he croaked. "Maybe I'm not fine after all." He lay back on the ground.

Cora rushed to the badger. "What is it?" she asked, concern filling her big blue eyes.

"My paw." The badger held out his front left paw and winced.

Isabelle gasped. "I'm so sorry, Mr Badger. I think I stepped on it!" She hung her head, feeling terrible.

"Please don't worry — it was my fault for not looking where I was going. I had my head in the treetops!" the badger said, still lying on the ground. "And do call me Bobby — Mr Badger makes me feel even older than I am!"

Bobby looked quite uncomfortable, Cora thought, with his face on the ground. "Why don't you come and lean against this tree stump," she said. She bent her head down so he could lean on her horn to hobble over. Bobby settled himself on the tree trunk and smiled.

"Thank you." He blinked again. "Three unicorns. Well I never!"

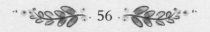

"What were you saying about the legend?" Isabelle asked.

Bobby's black eyes gleamed. "It was a tale my dear Auntie Bina used to tell me, when I was just a nipper."

"What was it?" Lei tried not to sound impatient. But she *really* wanted to understand what Bobby was talking about. "Please, can you tell it to us?"

"Let me see. You know, I think I can. I may be the oldest animal around these parts, but my memory doesn't usually let me down."

The unicorns held their breath as they waited for Bobby to tell his story.

"Auntie Bina told me there was a time – hundreds of years before she was born – when unicorns roamed Blossom Wood like any other animal," Bobby began in his deep voice. "She said there weren't many of them – just three or four – and they were shy creatures who lived in Echo Mountains."

Maybe that's where the hoof prints in the cave come from? thought Lei.

"But although they were shy, the unicorns helped the woodland greatly, because they had something the other

animals didn't. They were ... magical," Bobby said, his last word a whisper. "This magic was incredibly special, because each unicorn held a different kind of magic, meaning they could help the creatures here in different ways."

"What happened to them?" Isabelle asked.

Bobby closed his eyes. "Auntie Bina never said. It's why I never really believed the tale — she always liked making up stories and I thought this was just one of them." He opened his eyes again. "And then I met you."

"Wow," breathed Cora. She imagined being Bobby and thought she probably wouldn't have believed Auntie Bina either.

Isabelle tingled with excitement. "So if we're unicorns, are we magical too?"

Bobby shrugged. "Well, I wouldn't like to say. I still don't know how much of the legend is true. Have you felt any magic?"

"Our hooves!" Lei blurted out. "They make sparks when we move..."

Bobby's eyes widened. "Can you show me?"

The three cousins looked at each other. "Cora, you show Bobby," said Isabelle. "I think yours are the prettiest!"

Cora flicked her golden mane to one side and nodded, though she couldn't quite believe the sparks were magical. Magic was what she read about in books – not what she could do herself! She began prancing around, feeling the heat in her hooves as they hit the ground and made gold sparkles shimmer in the air.

"Keep going!" said Bobby, clapping his good paw against his knee. Cora started cantering, round and round and round in circles beside the tree stump where Bobby sat.

Lei and Isabelle watched on, their mouths gaping open, as more and more sparks flew. Hundreds turned to thousands, and Cora felt fizzing heat travelling up her legs and through her body. The warmth spread around her, and now sparks came from everywhere – all over her legs, body and chest. They were so bright, Cora looked like one giant golden sparkler.

Still cantering but not yet out of breath, Cora felt the heat travel into her neck, head and up into her horn, and she saw gold sparks fly from it, right in front of her eyes. Her head felt warm and dazzling, as if it was full of power she didn't know she had.

She stopped in front of Bobby and, without thinking about what she was doing, bent her head towards him. Cora felt the magic shooting from her horn into Bobby's paw, like tiny little bolts of electricity. What was happening?

Chapter 6
Cora's Magic

Cora's horn fizzed and tingled as she held still, while Bobby stared at the sparks flying into his paw. They seemed to disappear on impact, as if they were shimmering into his skin. But he didn't seem scared. In fact, he was smiling!

"It's better!" Bobby declared, leaping

up on to all fours as Cora pulled away
and the golden sparks died down. "My
paw!"

"Wh-at?" Cora said slowly, unable to
believe her eyes, or her ears.

"It's your magic." Bobby began
skipping around. He looked more like a
bouncy rabbit than an old badger now.
"You must be a healer!"

Lei and Isabelle crowded around Cora.
The golden sparks had disappeared now,

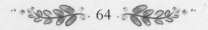

but Cora's white coat seemed to glimmer with magic. "Awesome ... that's just AWESOME!" Lei yelled, kicking out her front hooves in delight.

Bobby finally stopped dancing and sat back down. "My, I haven't done that in a long time," he panted. "But then, I haven't ever met unicorns before! Just wait until the woodlanders find out about you. They're going to be as happy as chestnuts!"

Cora beamed. She felt warm and

cosy inside, like she'd just drunk the most delicious and creamy hot chocolate. Then she remembered the other animals in Blossom Wood, and their reactions to them earlier. "But the other woodlanders are scared of us. They don't believe in unicorns," Cora told Bobby.

Bobby was quiet for a moment before he spoke. "Leave it with me. I might be able to fix that. Can you meet me in Foxglove Glade in an hour's time?"

Once Bobby had explained where the glade was – between Willow Lake and the Great Hedge – he hurried off. Lei, Isabelle and Cora looked at each other.

Cora suddenly gasped. "How will we know when an hour's passed?" Now that she was a unicorn, she didn't have her watch!

"Umm, we could count the seconds?"

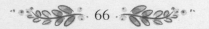

Isabelle suggested. "One Mississippi, two Mississippi, three Mississippi..."

Lei shook her pink mane. "We don't need to — I've got an idea!" She found a stick on the ground and rested it on a rock, so it rose up diagonally. Then she picked up some pebbles with her teeth and dropped them in a semicircle around the stick, nudging them into place with her nose.

Isabelle frowned. "What *are* you doing?"

Lei grinned, looked up at the sun, and then nodded. "It's a sundial! When the shadow from the stick reaches the next pebble, an hour will have passed."

Cora nickered. "That's so clever!"

"Thanks!" Lei said, hoping the hour would pass quickly. She was excited to see what Bobby had in store!

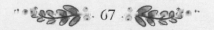

As soon as the sundial's shadow touched the little grey pebble, the cousins began galloping through the forest. "Where is everybody?" Cora wondered as her powerful hooves hit the ground and she felt the energy ripple through her body. Whereas before the creatures had run away from them, now there weren't any at all!

"I think I know," Lei replied, tilting her

ears forward. She could hear the chattering of what sounded like thousands of animals.

"Oh, it's beautiful!" Isabelle had spotted Foxglove Glade up ahead. The foxglove flowers around it seemed to be every colour of the rainbow. As the sun's rays hit the flowers, they lit up like the most beautiful fairy lights.

Cora skidded to a stop. "But there are so many creatures there." She could

see every sort of woodland animal, from tiny bees to towering bears. "Are they all waiting for us?"

"Yes, indeed they are," came a familiar gravelly voice, and Bobby stepped out into the path. "But please don't worry, I have a plan. Promise to trust me?"

"We promise," the three cousins replied solemnly.

"Marvellous. Can you wait here until I call you?"

The unicorns nodded and Bobby disappeared back into the crowd of animals in the glade. Lei tapped her hooves as she waited, while Cora flared her nostrils nervously. Then they heard Bobby call for quiet, and Isabelle flicked her ears up to catch what he was saying:

"Mo, would you come and join me, please?"

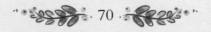

Lei, Cora and Isabelle looked out from behind a large tree trunk and saw Bobby standing at one end of the glade, which sloped upwards, like a stage.

A squeak shot out from the crowd, and the unicorns saw a little mouse scurrying towards Bobby.

Bobby bent his head down towards Mo. "Am I right that you've had terrible earache this week?"

Mo nodded and pressed his tiny paws to his ears. "Not even hot nettle milk has helped them."

"I have an idea," Bobby told the mouse. "But you must not be scared." He looked up at the entire crowd of animals. "You too – there's no need to be frightened."

Cora began to tremble. She guessed what Bobby was about to do. Sure

enough, he cupped his paws to his mouth and called, "Cora, please can you come to the stage?"

"Go on," said Isabelle gently, while Lei nudged Cora with her nose.

"We promised Bobby," Lei whispered. "Go!"

Cora took a long, deep breath. She moved one hoof, then another, trotting slowly towards the glade. As she came out from the shadows, the crowd gasped as one. Cora trotted carefully around the animals, very aware of the golden sparks shooting up from her hooves as she moved between them.

Bobby gave Cora a giant grin as she reached the stage. He looked relieved. "This is Cora," he told Mo. "She's a unicorn, and she's going to help you."

Mo stared up at Cora, his tiny eyes

wide with disbelief. "B–but unicorns aren't real…" His voice was the quietest squeak Cora had ever heard.

"I promise you, they are," said Bobby. "Cora, can you show Mo your magic?"

Cora gave a little snort of panic, but tried not to think about everyone watching. She began to trot in circles around Bobby and Mo, feeling the heat rising into her hooves and her legs. She didn't need to look down to know that her magic sparks were flying, slowly covering her body, her neck and her head as the warmth rose through her. As she felt it fizz into her horn, she bent down carefully towards the little mouse and touched his ears, one after another, with the very tip. Sparks shot out of her horn as the crowd watched in silence.

All this time, Mo hadn't moved, but as

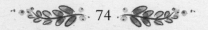

soon as Cora raised her head, the mouse jumped for joy. "It's a miracle!" he squealed, kicking his legs together in the air. "My ears don't hurt at all now!"

Whispers of excitement buzzed around the crowd, building into a huge roar of applause. "She IS a unicorn!" everyone cheered, clapping their wings, hooves and paws together in great excitement. Meanwhile, Bobby beckoned to Isabelle and Lei.

As they trotted up to the stage, the woodlanders grew quiet again, watching the unicorns in awe.

"There are more of them?" Mo squeaked.

"They're beautiful!" squealed a caterpillar, as everyone's excited chatter filled the glade.

"Well done," Isabelle whispered as they

joined Cora, and her chest swelled with pride.

Bobby clapped his paws together. "So you see, everyone, the legend was true. Unicorns are real. Their magic is real!"

"Three cheers for the unicorns!" yelled a squirrel at the front. "Hip hip, HOORAY!"

"Hip hip, HOORAY!" everyone joined in. "Hip hip, HOORAY!"

Suddenly, the animals, birds and insects all crowded around the unicorns, wanting to say hello and introduce themselves. *What a turnaround!* thought Lei, as they met the cheering squirrel, who was called Loulou, and the excited caterpillar named Wilf.

Sara, a deer, apologized for running away from them earlier that day. "I hope you'll forgive me," she said in a silky voice. "I just couldn't believe my eyes!"

"Will you stay for a bite to eat?" Bobby asked with a beam.

As he said it, Lei's stomach rumbled. They'd been on such an adventure, but they hadn't eaten a thing!

The barbie! Cora remembered. "We'd love to, but we've got dinner waiting for us," she told Bobby gently.

Isabelle and Lei quickly realized what she meant. "Sorry, Bobby, but we'll be back very soon," Isabelle promised.

"I sincerely hope so, unicorns. You have made an old badger VERY happy!"

They said goodbye to all of the woodlanders — by which time Lei's stomach with growling with hunger — then flicked their ears and trotted away. "I can't believe we're in Blossom Wood AND we're unicorns AND we have magical powers!" Cora glanced down at the golden sparks at her feet and neighed happily.

"I know!" Lei beamed. "So if you're a healer, Cora," she added, "I wonder what magic I have..."

"And me!" Isabelle cried, breaking into a canter as they neared the mountains. "I can't wait to find out!"

For now, the cousins were going home. But they would keep their promise to Bobby, that was for sure. They'd be back to the wonderful Blossom Wood for more magical adventures just as soon as they could!

Did You Know?

❀ Just as Cora says in the story, the best way to move towards a deer is in a zigzag. This way, the animal thinks you're just another deer, and not about to attack them.

❀ Mice squeak a lot when they're scared or hurt. But they also squeak when they're happy, too!

❀ Bears really do like to climb trees. Their claws help them to get up the trunk!

❀ Like the unicorns, horses have springy hooves that help them gallop fast.

Spot The Difference

Can you spot five things that are different in these pictures?

Which Unicorn Are You?

Take this quiz to find out!

1 – What is your favourite colour?

a)   Red

b)   Purple

c)   Pink

2 – What is your favourite subject at school?

a)   Drama

b)   English

c)   Science

3 – What do you like doing most?

a)   Gymnastics

b)   Swimming

c)   Inventing things

4 – What would be your perfect snack?

a)   Crisps

b)   Strawberries

c)   Chocolate biscuits

5 – Which country would you like to live in?

a)   England

b)   Australia

c)   America

Mostly As: You are Isabelle! You love to daydream and have a brilliant imagination. You often make up stories for your friends – and sometimes even act them out!

Mostly Bs: You are Cora! You love swimming and listening to music and you often have your head in a book. Your honestly and loyalty makes you a very good friend.

Mostly Cs: You are Lei! You love learning new facts and discovering things about the world. You are passionate and determined to get things done – but you always make time for your friends.

Cora Fact File

In this story, Cora discovers her healing magic. Here are some other fun facts about Cora.

Name: Cora Williams

Age: 9

Family: Lives with her mum and dad (no brothers or sisters)

Home town: Sydney, New South Wales, Australia

Pets: A cat called Button

Favourite drink: Strawberry milkshake

Favourite word: Ace

Favourite book: *Bambi* by Felix Salten, *The Magic Faraway Tree* by Enid Blyton and *Matilda* by Roald Dahl (too many favourites to choose one!)

Likes: Listening to music, reading, swimming, baking

Dislikes: Being the centre of attention

❀ Would you like more animal
fun and facts?

❀ Fancy flying across the treetops in
a magical Blossom Wood game?

❀ Want sneak peeks of other
books in the series?

Then check out the
Blossom Wood website at:

blossomwoodbooks.com

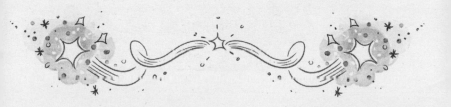

Meet

The Owls of Blossom Wood

in these magical books

Turn over for a
sneak peek of another

The
Unicorns of
Blossom Wood

adventure!

Catherine Coe

Unicorn games
& quizzes
inside!

The
Unicorns of
Blossom Wood
❧ Festival Time ❧

Chapter 1

Let It Snow

Pat, pat, pat. Patter, patter, patter.

Isabelle yawned and snuggled down further in her sleeping bag. The rain pattering on the tent had woken her up, but she wasn't ready to start the day yet. She was cosy and warm, lying in between her two cousins, Lei and Cora. They were still fast asleep – Lei snoring gently and Cora curled up in a ball so all Isabelle could see was her silky blonde hair. Isabelle wondered whether to wake them, but they looked so peaceful that she decided not to. Instead she pulled out her notebook and pen from under her pillow.

"Blossom Wood is the most beautiful place I've ever seen," she started to write. "It's so amazing it feels like a dream. . ."

She stopped suddenly. Maybe it *was* just a dream. Yesterday, Isabelle had thought that she and her cousins had been transported to a magical wood where they were no longer girls, but unicorns! But Isabelle always had very vivid dreams. Maybe this was just one of them? Her heart felt heavy — she'd be so disappointed if it wasn't real and they couldn't go back again. Now she couldn't wait any longer for Lei and Cora to wake up.

Isabelle gently shook their shoulders. Lei yelled, "Argh, what's happening?" while Cora uncurled and flashed open her blue eyes.

"Sorry!" said Isabelle, her heart pounding with worry now. "But I need to know something. Did I dream Blossom Wood, or was it real?"

Lei beamed, and her dark brown eyes twinkled. "It was real," she replied, nodding furiously.

Cora grinned too. "We turned into unicorns, we really did!"

Isabelle hugged both her cousins at once as relief flooded through her.

"Now, since you woke me up, I have a question for you," Lei said, leaping up from her sleeping bag. "When are we going back?"

Isabelle looked down at her purple checked pyjamas. "Um, we probably need to get dressed first!" she said. They'd got to Blossom Wood by stepping into some hoof prints in a nearby cove, but they couldn't really leave the campsite in their sleeping gear... What would they tell their parents?

Lei pulled her long, dark hair into a ponytail, revealing the pink braids in her hair underneath. She grabbed her towel. "Come on then! Last one to the shower block has to clean up the tent!"

"But we're meant to be going on a hike today, remember," said Cora, the smile disappearing from her face. The three families were on holiday together – even though Cora lived in Australia, Isabelle in England and Lei in the USA, they always met up for a week or two during the summer holidays.

Lei unzipped the tent and looked out. "Yeah, but it's raining! Hopefully the hike will get cancelled."

Isabelle nodded, making her red

curls bounce about. She'd been looking forward to walking around the valleys here, but there was no way it'd be as good as another visit to Blossom Wood!

After they'd showered and dressed, they found their parents sitting on camping chairs under the awning of Lei's parents' tent. Isabelle's mum was handing out mugs, while Lei's dad set up their portable stove. Lei's older sister, Ying, lay on her back across the tarpaulin – headphones in, eyes shut, nodding her head to her music.

Cora's mum stared out at the rain, shaking her head. "Looks like the hike is off, girls. According to the forecast, it's going to rain all day."

Lei tried to look disappointed, but her insides bubbled with hope. Now they just had to figure out a reason to go down to

the cove with the hoof prints...

Lei's mum held up a guidebook. "There's a local café in here — it says they do the best cream cakes for miles, *and* they have an art gallery."

Lei's dad looked up from the stove. "Do they do tea and coffee too? I can't get this stove to work, no matter what I do!"

"Yes," his wife replied with a smile. "A selection of hot and cold drinks, according to this, plus pastries and doughnuts."

Cora's dad patted his stomach. "Sounds ace. Shall we have brekkie there then?"

The adults all nodded and got up from their chairs. "Get your umbrellas, girls," said Lei's mum. "It's about a ten-minute walk."

"Um ... I'm not really hungry," said Isabelle.

"Me neither," added Lei.

Isabelle's mum raised her eyebrows. "You don't want cakes for breakfast?"

They shook their heads. "I'm still stuffed from the barbie last night," said Cora, which was true, although cakes did sound good. Just not as good as becoming a unicorn!

"Can we stay here?" Lei asked. "Ying will keep an eye on us, won't you, Ying?"

Ying opened one eye, nodded, then closed it again.

"If you're sure," said Lei's dad. "I guess sitting in a café isn't very exciting. Just don't go too far from the campsite, OK?"

"We won't." Isabelle linked arms with Cora and Lei. It wasn't really a lie, because the hoof prints were close by. But of course Blossom Wood was a whole different world entirely!

Five minutes later, Lei, Cora and Isabelle were running down the hill from their campsite towards a small blue lake. They weren't going far, just like they'd promised – down to a little cove at the side of the lake. And they knew no time would pass back here while they were away in Blossom Wood.

Their trainers squelched in the muddy ground and raindrops splattered on their faces, but they didn't mind. Soon they reached the sandy shore, and they sprinted into the cove – which was like a shallow cave in the hillside surrounded by pretty flowers.

"They're still there!" gasped Cora. She'd been worrying that the three sets of hoof prints in the rocky ground might have disappeared somehow. She jumped

into the ones that matched her feet —
the biggest set — while Lei stepped into
the smallest prints and Isabelle into the
medium-sized ones.

Dazzling white light filled the cove,
making the girls close their eyes. "We're
going to Blossom Wood!" yelled Lei, as

warmth shot through her feet and into her legs, body and arms.

"And we'll soon be unicorns!" added Isabelle, smiling as she felt hot tingles dance across her skin.

Cora trembled as the warm magic flooded through her. Before yesterday, she didn't even believe in magic, but now she was about to become a unicorn!

Sure enough, when the bright light faded and Cora opened her eyes, she saw shiny hooves where her feet used to be, and white unicorn legs instead of her normal two. When she looked up, she shrieked. Blossom Wood lay before her like last time they'd visited, but now there was one big difference: it was covered in sparkling snow.